Anna Maria's Gift

Anna Maria's Gift

by *Janice Shefelman*
illustrated by *Robert Papp*

A STEPPING STONE BOOK™
Random House New York

For my one and only Tom —J.S.

Published in the United States by Random House Children's Books, a division of Random House, Inc., New York. Originally published in hardcover in the United States by Random House Children's Books, New York, in 2010.

Random House and the colophon are registered trademarks and A Stepping Stone Book and the colophon are trademarks of Random House, Inc.

Visit us on the Web! www.randomhouse.com/kids

Educators and librarians, for a variety of teaching tools, visit us at www.randomhouse.com/teachers

The Library of Congress has cataloged the hardcover edition of this work as follows:
Shefelman, Janice Jordan.
Anna Maria's gift / by Janice Shefelman ; illustrated by Robert Papp.
p. cm.
"A Stepping Stone Book."
Summary: In 1715 Italy, nine-year-old Anna Maria Lombardini arrives at a Venice orphanage with little but the special violin her father made for her, but when her teacher, Antonio Vivaldi, favors her over a fellow student, the beloved instrument winds up in a canal. Includes glossary and historical note.
ISBN 978-0-375-85881-9 (trade) — ISBN 978-0-375-95881-6 (lib. bdg.) — ISBN 978-0-375-85882-6 (pbk.)
[1. Violin—Fiction. 2. Orphans—Fiction. 3. Vivaldi, Antonio, 1678–1741—Fiction. 4. Conduct of life—Fiction. 5. Schools—Fiction. 6. Venice (Italy)—History—1508–1797—Fiction. 7. Italy—History—1559–1789—Fiction.]
I. Papp, Robert, ill. II. Title.
PZ7.S54115Ann 2010 [Fic]—dc22 2009004553

Printed in the United States of America 10 9 8 7 6 5 4 3 2 1

Random House Children's Books supports the First Amendment and celebrates the right to read.

Contents

1.
A Promise

Cremona, Italy
1715

On a cold February afternoon, Anna Maria lay on her bed, crying. Snow fell outside the window. It covered the balcony and the narrow street below.

Sister Bianca, Papa's nurse, came to the door. "Hush, child." She had a frown on her thin face. "Your father wants a last word with you."

Terror pierced Anna Maria's heart. "Is Papa going to die?"

"He will enter the Kingdom of Heaven," said the sister.

"No! I want him to stay here." Anna Maria bolted out her door and hurried down the dark hall. The sound of Papa's coughing came from his room. It was the same cough that had taken Mama away last year.

Anna Maria smoothed her blond curls back and wiped her eyes. Then she opened the door and looked in. A candle burned on the table beside the big bed.

Papa lay propped up on pillows. Anna Maria stared at the side of his face. His long, pointed nose was like a beak.

Then she ran to his bed. "Papa!"

He turned his head toward her and his eyes shone. "Annina, my angel."

"Papa, don't leave me!" She clasped his hand. It was rough and stained from making violins.

"You will not be alone, Annina. I have made a new violin for you," he said. "Go and look in my workshop."

Anna Maria did not move. She had to hold on to Papa.

"Quickly now, bring it to me," he urged.

Anna Maria ran down the stairs and across the snowy courtyard. In his workshop, a new violin case lay on the bench. She picked it up and hurried back. Opening the lid, she lifted the violin out of the case. Its golden wood glowed as if lit from within.

"Oh, Papa, how beautiful."

"There is an inscription inside," he said.

She held the violin to the light and read.

For Annina
Play and you shall hear my voice
Nicolo Lombardini
Made in the Year 1715

"It is true," Papa said. "I kept the violin here in my room for a month before varnishing it. And while I slept, my soul entered its body." He paused to gather strength. "Sister Bianca will take you to live at the Pietà in Venice."

Anna Maria shook her head. That was a home for orphan girls. "I don't want to go, Papa. I want to stay with you."

"You cannot stay with me, Annina." He took her hand. "Your mother was happy there when she was a girl. And so was Sister Bianca."

Anna Maria kept shaking her head while Papa had a coughing spell. She could not imagine Sister Bianca being happy anywhere.

At last he went on. "Antonio Vivaldi will be your violin teacher."

"But I like Maestro Cavalli," said Anna Maria.

Papa held up his hand for silence. "He is a good teacher. But Don Vivaldi is a great one. Do you remember when he came here to buy a violin? You played for him. He said you were a most talented child."

Anna Maria remembered, even though she was only five years old then. Now she was nine, and everything was changing.

"But, Papa, I don't want you to leave me," she said.

"Annina, my angel. As long as you have your violin, I will be with you. And you will be safe at the Pietà." He touched the violin. "Now, play for me. The largo from Vivaldi's D Minor Concerto. You know, *dum dee-dee dum.*"

Anna Maria knew. After tuning, she tucked the violin under her chin. Then she closed her eyes and drew the bow across the strings. She let herself be carried along by

the music and the sweet, clear voice of the violin. Papa's voice.

After the last note, Papa reached out and touched her cheek. "You have such talent, Annina. Promise me you will go to the Pietà and study with Don Vivaldi."

Anna Maria bit her lips together and nodded. Invisible hands seemed to be gripping her throat. She could not speak.

2. Venice

After Papa died, Anna Maria and Sister Bianca traveled across country by carriage. They left Cremona far behind and with it everything that was dear—except her violin. But even with Papa's violin beside her, there was an ache in Anna Maria's chest. It felt as if her heart had cracked.

She turned to Sister Bianca. "Papa told me you lived at the Pietà when you were a girl. What is it like?" Anna Maria asked.

Sister Bianca answered without looking at her. "You will be safe from the outside world."

Anna Maria stared at Sister Bianca's narrow face and tight mouth. "You mean the girls can't go out?"

"No," said the sister.

Anna Maria leaned back. "Then I don't want to go there."

"You have no choice," Sister Bianca said. "You should be thankful to have Don Vivaldi for a violin teacher."

It was Papa's last wish. No matter how awful the Pietà might be, she must keep her promise. Anna Maria hugged the violin case. *I will make my violin sing with your voice, Papa.*

On the fourth day, they came to a fishing village at the edge of a wide lagoon. Several gondolas were tied up at the dock, waiting for passengers. The driver stopped, opened the door, and lowered the steps.

Anna Maria climbed out. She gazed at the island of Venice across the lagoon. The setting sun made it look like a golden lily pad sprouting domes and towers.

"Look, Sister, Venice floats on the water!"

"Don't be silly, child," Sister Bianca said. "It stands on thousands of posts set in the bottom of the lagoon."

Anna Maria preferred the floating idea.

Sister Bianca held the violin case in one hand. "See now, you forgot your violin. You must be more careful."

Anna Maria gasped and took the case. "Oh, how could I?"

"That is easy," one of the gondoliers called. "You were dazzled by Venice!" He walked up and bowed. His dark hair curled from under his red cap. "Good day. My name is Francesco. Step into my floating palace, and I will take you there on a song." His eyes sparked with good humor.

Sister Bianca gave him a sour look. "How much?"

"For you, half fare—only six *lire,*" he answered with a smile.

The sister nodded. "To the Pietà."

"*Sì,*" Francesco said, "where the orphan girls live." He paused. "You are an orphan, *signorina*?"

Anna Maria looked down.

"Ah, but you cannot be sad in Venice—especially during Carnival. It is not allowed!" He offered his hand to help her aboard. "Hold tight to your violin. We don't want it to fall into the lagoon."

Inside the cabin they sat on red velvet cushions. Anna Maria laid the violin case across her lap.

Francesco steered the boat out into the lagoon. "I promised you a song. So here is one to make you laugh. It is called 'Macaroni Rain.'" He leaned into the oar and began to sing as he rowed.

"If macaroni rained down from the sky,
And the earth were covered over with cheese,
We'd use our oars as forks, you and I.
How jolly! Macaroni raining down
from the sky!"

Anna Maria laughed for the first time since Papa died.

"*Signorina,* if you play your violin for me, this ride is free," Francesco said.

Anna Maria could not resist. She took out her violin and played the song back to him.

"*Brava!* Not many girls could do that," said Francesco. "You will be Don Vivaldi's prize pupil."

"I hope so," Anna Maria said, feeling happier already. "Let's do the macaroni song again, together."

This time he sang along with her. Afterward they both laughed. Even Sister Bianca smiled. *Perhaps it is true that no one can be sad here,* thought Anna Maria.

When they drew close to Venice, Francesco said, "*Signorina,* open the curtains. We are entering the one and only Grand Canal."

Anna Maria pushed them back and

looked from side to side. Marble palaces lined the canal. Chandeliers glittered in the windows. The gondola floated along silently. In the twilight it felt like they were no longer attached to the earth.

The Grand Canal wound through Venice and came out into a wide basin. "The Basin of San Marco," Francesco said. He waved his arm to the left. "And there, San Marco Basilica, the bell tower, and the palace of the doge."

"Hmph. The bell tower is not as tall as ours in Cremona," Sister Bianca whispered.

But Anna Maria did not listen. She gazed at the sights—the domes of San Marco, the lacy arches of the palace, and the black gondolas swarming around.

Francesco rowed along the bank where there was a broad sidewalk. The Riva, he called it. People strolled to and fro, greeting one another. Many wore strange white masks with beak noses. Anna Maria shuddered. They looked like death heads. Still, everyone seemed happy. A few people were throwing painted eggs, and one hit Francesco.

He laughed. "It is only filled with perfumed water. This is Carnival, Venice-style."

Soon they came to a tall pink building. "Here we are, *signorina.* Your new home." Francesco tied the gondola beside the steps and helped them out.

Anna Maria stood holding her violin case and looked up. The Pietà was five stories tall. It stretched from one canal to the next.

She thought of her home on the narrow street in Cremona, with its friendly windows and balconies. Here the windows were tightly shuttered. No, this was not home.

Francesco picked up their bags and started toward the door. "Make way, my friends,

make way for Don Vivaldi's prize pupil!" he called.

A man wearing a cape of red feathers bowed as they passed.

The sound of a violin came from a window above the door. It was the most energetic, wild playing she had ever heard.

"Only two people can play the violin like that," said Francesco. "Vivaldi and the devil!"

Anna Maria put her hand over her mouth to hide a smile. *Can he teach me to play like the devil?* she wondered.

Sister Bianca stiffened and glared at Francesco.

"Excuse me, Sister, but it is true."

Then Francesco lifted the door knocker. He let it fall three times. The hollow sound made Anna Maria's smile fade. She pulled her cloak tighter around her. It felt like she was entering a prison, never to come out again.

3. The Pietà

A young nun opened the door and peered at them by the light of her lantern.

"I am Sister Bianca, and this is Anna Maria, an orphan. The prioress is expecting us."

The nun nodded, waving them inside.

Anna Maria picked up her bag and looked at Francesco. "Farewell, *signore.*"

"Remember to eat lots of macaroni and cheese," he said.

Anna Maria tried to smile, but her lips quivered.

"If you ever need me, my station is there." Francesco pointed to a bridge over the next canal.

Before Anna Maria could answer, the nun closed the door. She bolted and locked it with a final clank. They crossed the empty parlor, their steps echoing on the stone floor.

Light from the lantern flashed on the iron bars that covered all the windows. Anna Maria wanted to turn and run out the door. How could she ever be happy in this prison? Francesco was wrong.

A door opened and light poured out around a large, white-robed figure.

"Ah, you must be Anna Maria," said the figure. "Welcome to your new home. I am Mother Elena, the prioress." She embraced Anna Maria and then Sister Bianca.

"It is good to see you after such a long time, Bianca. Come, sit by the fire and warm yourselves." Mother Elena turned to the young nun. "Sister Camilla, please have the kitchen send coffee and chocolate."

"But, Mother, it is time for vespers," said the nun.

"It's all right. They need warmth more than the word of God right now." Mother Elena's smile and her plump, rosy cheeks made Anna Maria feel warmer already.

Camilla returned with a tray. Mother Elena excused her, saying, "Send Silvia to me after vespers."

Anna Maria sipped her chocolate and listened. The two women talked of a time when they were girls at the Pietà together. The years seemed to melt away in the warmth of the fire, and they became young again.

By and by there was a knock on the door.

A girl dressed in a red uniform entered. Her face was scarred by smallpox, but her dark eyes glittered like jewels.

"Silvia, this is Anna Maria, our new resident," said the prioress. "Please show her to the dormitory."

Then Mother Elena spoke to Anna Maria. "Tomorrow Sister Lidia will take you to your lessons. She is to be your guardian, or your aunt, as we say here."

Silvia took Anna Maria's bag. She led the way along the gallery that opened onto a courtyard. "You have your own violin?"

"*Sì,* my father made it for me. What do *you* play?" Anna Maria asked.

"The cello. It's my best friend," Silvia replied.

Anna Maria smiled. She liked Silvia already.

At the end of the gallery, they came to a

spiral staircase. They climbed up and up to the fourth floor.

Anna Maria looked over the balcony railing to the courtyard below. "I've never slept so far off the ground."

"It's all I have ever known," said Silvia, stopping at a door. "I think you'll like it here, especially Maestro Vivaldi. Just don't mind Paolina."

Before Anna Maria could ask her who Paolina was, Silvia opened the door. The long room had two rows of beds. Nearby, a group of girls turned to look at Anna Maria.

"Are you the new orphan?" a tall, slender girl asked.

Anna Maria nodded. But the word was like a knife in her heart. *This must be . . .*

"My name is Paolina of the Violin," the tall girl said. "What is yours?"

"Anna Maria Lombardini."

"Ah! Did you hear that, girls? She has a real name—not an instrument for a name like the rest of us." Paolina put her nose in the air. "That makes her better than we are."

"No, that's not true," Anna Maria said. "I'm an orphan, just like you."

Silvia took Anna Maria by the hand and led her past the group.

"You must be rich to have your own violin," Paolina called after them.

Silvia stopped and turned. "You're just jealous, Paolina."

"Of what, scar face?" Paolina jeered.

Silvia's eyes sharpened with hate, but she did not answer.

Just then the supper bell rang. Paolina and her group left.

"She's worried that you might become Maestro Vivaldi's favorite instead of her," Silvia said. "He told us you were very talented."

"She's very cruel." Anna Maria hated Paolina already.

Silvia nodded. "She has her following, but I'm not one of them. I would rather play my cello."

"That's how I feel about my violin," said Anna Maria. "Playing music makes me forget everything else."

"Me too." Silvia paused and looked

down. "I'm sorry you lost your father." Then, looking at Anna Maria, she said, "I never even knew mine. Tell me, what is it like, having a father?"

Anna Maria could not think what to say. It was hard enough to lose a father. But never to have had one was even worse. She let her mind drift back to Cremona, to Papa in his workshop. Remembering brought a lump to her throat.

"My father loved making violins." She paused and swallowed. "But whenever I went into his workshop, he forgot them. As if I were his favorite violin." Anna Maria blinked to keep back the tears.

"Thank you." Silvia put her hand on Anna Maria's arm. "Now I understand."

At the far end of the room, Silvia set the bag down. "This is your bed next to mine—and a long way from Paolina's."

"Good," Anna Maria said. She looked at the red uniform laid out there.

"That's for tomorrow," Silvia said. "Now it's time for supper."

Anna Maria put her violin case in the trunk at the foot of the bed. Then she followed Silvia out.

The dining room was on the ground floor between the front and back courtyards. Logs blazed in the fireplaces at each end. Candles lit the rows of long tables. *A cheerful place,* Anna Maria thought, *but so quiet.*

"No talking in here," Silvia whispered.

After the blessing, everyone ate in silence while a nun read from the Bible. Anna Maria barely heard the words or tasted the bean soup. She wanted to be home, having supper with Papa. He would tell her about a violin he was making. And Anna Maria would tell him what she had learned at the convent school that day. Or about her violin lesson with Maestro Cavalli. *If only everything could be like it was,* she thought.

Later, all the girls knelt by their beds to pray. Then one of the sisters snuffed out the candles. Anna Maria crawled into bed.

From the Riva below she could hear the music and laughter of Carnival celebrations. Here in the dark room there were eleven other girls lying in their beds. But she was more alone than ever.

Anna Maria crept to the end of the bed and opened her trunk. She took her violin out of its case. Then she pulled the covers over the two of them.

4.
First Lesson

At sunrise the chapel bell rang. Silvia and the other girls began to stir. They said the morning prayer as they dressed in the chill air. "Hail Mary, full of grace . . ."

Anna Maria slipped out of bed and put her violin back in the trunk. She glanced around to see if anyone noticed. Her heart fell. Paolina was watching with a smirk on her face, even while she said the prayer.

Anna Maria pulled the red uniform over

her head. The cloth was rough and scratchy. It made her feel like an orphan.

The other girls were dressed and standing at the foot of their beds. A nun waited silently at the door. Anna Maria pulled the blanket over her pillow and stepped into her place. Then the nun led them downstairs to the chapel.

Anna Maria bent her knee, signed the cross, and sat down next to Silvia. Along one side of the chapel there was a deep balcony.

"That's where we perform," Silvia whispered.

Perform! The word sent a thrill of excitement through Anna Maria. She imagined playing her violin up there for all the world to hear. Maybe there *was* something good about living in this place.

After Mass, the nun led them into the dining room for chocolate and rolls. There was no talking at breakfast, either.

Anna Maria looked up and down the table at the other girls. They had ways of talking silently. Mouthed words, rolled eyes, a tilt of the head, an elbow nudge. Paolina was making fun of her. She pretended to play a violin. Then she hugged it and closed her eyes.

Anna Maria turned to Silvia and mouthed the words *I hate her.* Silvia nodded.

Three bells rang. The girls stood and filed out, table by table. At the door a nun smiled and called her over.

"I am Sister Lidia, your aunt here. Welcome to the Pietà, dear child."

Anna Maria could only stare. Sister Lidia's pale skin and gentle blue eyes stirred up a vivid memory.

"Are you thinking that I look like your mother?" Sister Lidia asked.

Anna Maria was surprised. "How did you know?"

"Because your mother and I were best friends here. Everyone said we could be sisters. And who knows? Maybe we were."

Anna Maria flung her arms around Sister Lidia. "You are truly my aunt. I know you are!"

"Perhaps so, dear child." Sister Lidia took Anna Maria by the shoulders. "It is time for your class with Maestro Vivaldi. Go fetch your violin, and I'll meet you on the first floor."

Anna Maria ran and got her violin. Sister Lidia led the way to the music room. As girls entered and sat down, she took Anna Maria to meet the maestro.

He stood at the front of the room, dressed in a priest's black robe. His red hair sprang out from under his cap like curling flames of fire. The Red Priest, he was called.

"Maestro Vivaldi, this is Anna Maria Lombardini," Sister Lidia said.

"Daughter of the violin maker!" He paused, and his eyes grew serious. "I am sorry to hear of his passing, my dear. He had many violins yet to give the world."

Anna Maria looked down, clutching her violin case.

"Could that be one of them?" he asked.

She looked up at him. "*Sì,* Maestro."

"Will you play it for us?"

Anna Maria nodded and took the violin out of the case. "This was my father's favorite piece."

She closed her eyes and began to play the largo from Maestro Vivaldi's own concerto. *Dum dee-dee dum.* As Anna Maria played, she was no longer in the music room. She was standing beside Papa's bed. She played with

all the sadness in her heart and heard his voice. *Beautiful, Annina, beautiful.*

When she finished, there was complete silence. She opened her eyes and saw the maestro looking at her, nodding.

"Thank you, my dear. Your teacher in Cremona lost an excellent student. I welcome you to our class." He reached out his hand. "May I look at the instrument?"

Anna Maria gave him the violin. He turned it over and back and read the inscription inside.

"Now I understand why it has such a sweet yet powerful voice." He handed the violin back. "You may sit here," he said, "next to Paolina."

The hate in Paolina's face took Anna Maria's breath away.

Maestro Vivaldi picked up his violin and bow. "Today, dear girls, we shall work on fingering. The music is before you—a lively little piece of mine. Try to keep the tips of your fingers upright."

He tucked the violin under his chin. "I will show you." He inhaled through his large hooked nose and attacked. His bow rocked up and down. His fingers galloped about like a spider.

Thoughts of Paolina flew out of Anna Maria's head. She did not know it was possible to play the violin that way. She vowed to learn how.

5.

Night Visitor

After a few days, Anna Maria knew the routine. Mass every morning and prayers seven times a day. In between were violin class, reading and grammar, arithmetic, religion, study, and practice. Violin classes with the maestro carried her through all the rest.

Today the girls were working on their staccato—playing short, quick notes. Suddenly Maestro Vivaldi rapped on the music stand with his bow.

"No, no, no!" he said, shaking his red curls. "Dear girls, you must relax your arm between strokes. I want *ta-ta-ta,* not *ahhh-ahhh-ahhh."*

The girls giggled.

"Only Anna Maria is doing it correctly." He looked at her. "Would you stand and demonstrate, my dear?"

Her heart leaped with pleasure. She stood, faced the class, and glanced at Paolina. The sneer on her face made Anna Maria pause.

"Is something wrong?" Maestro Vivaldi asked.

Anna Maria shook Paolina out of her head. "No, Maestro."

With her bow over the violin, she took a quick breath. Stroke, relax, stroke, relax. Her bow bounced on the strings.

"Brava," said Maestro Vivaldi. He turned to the rest of the girls. "Did you hear how

each stroke was separate—not slurred?"

Anna Maria took her seat and felt hate radiating from Paolina. It ruined the maestro's praise.

That afternoon Anna Maria sat down in the empty courtyard to practice. It was a clear March day. The sun warmed the walls and paving stones. Maestro Vivaldi had given her a violin piece to work on. She placed the music beside her and began to play.

After the final note, she realized that she was not alone. Sister Lidia sat on the other end of the bench.

"Oh, Auntie, I didn't see you," said Anna Maria.

"You were quite intent," Sister Lidia said. "From what Maestro Vivaldi tells me, you are his most promising pupil."

Anna Maria nodded without smiling. "I think Paolina hates me for that."

"*Sì,* maybe so," said the sister. "But you must love her in return."

Anna Maria shook her head. "I am not that good, Auntie. I love you, and I love

Maestro Vivaldi. But I could never love Paolina."

"You must try, Anna Maria. Jesus said to love one another."

"He never knew Paolina!" Anna Maria said.

Sister Lidia smiled, but it was not a joke.

Late that night while everyone slept, a shadowy figure crept to the foot of Anna Maria's bed. It opened the trunk, took the violin case, and tiptoed out the door.

6.
A Fight

At first light Anna Maria woke and saw that her trunk was open. She crawled to the foot of the bed and looked in.

"Someone has taken my violin!" she cried.

Girls sat up in bed. Silvia rushed over and peered in the trunk. "It's true. Is this someone's cruel joke?"

Anna Maria saw the smirk on Paolina's face. "You took it!" she screamed. "I know you did." With rage pounding in her chest, Anna Maria ran to Paolina's bed.

"Where are you hiding it?" She flung open Paolina's trunk and began throwing clothes out. No violin there.

Paolina jumped out of bed and shoved Anna Maria to the floor. "You stop that. I didn't touch your precious violin."

Anna Maria scrambled up. She threw herself at Paolina and grabbed a handful of stringy black hair. "Give it back, or I'll pull your hair out!"

Paolina took hold of Anna Maria's arm and sank her teeth into it. Sharp pain shot up to her shoulder. But Anna Maria did not let go.

Sister Lidia appeared at the door. "Stop, stop now!" She rushed to the girls and pulled them apart. "Your arm is bleeding, Anna Maria. What happened?"

"She stole my violin, Auntie. Make her give it back," said Anna Maria.

Sister Lidia looked at Paolina. "Is that true?"

"No, why would I want it, Sister? Maestro Vivaldi lets me play one of his own," Paolina said.

The chapel bell began ringing.

Sister Lidia glanced about the room. "Girls, time for your prayers. Mother Elena will decide what to do about this."

The other girls began murmuring their prayers. But they all watched to see what Sister Lidia would do.

"You two girls get dressed and come with me," she said. "Anna Maria, wash your arm first."

Anna Maria cried silently as she washed the blood from her arm. It stung, but she did not care. She wanted to wash Paolina's spit off her skin. Most of all, she wanted her violin back.

The two girls dressed and followed Sister Lidia downstairs. When the prioress opened the door, Anna Maria could not contain herself.

"Paolina stole my violin, Mother Elena! My father's gift," she said.

The prioress gasped. "Did you, Paolina?"

The girl shook her head and looked down.

"She did!" Anna Maria said. "She hates me, and I hate her."

Mother Elena put her finger on her lips for silence. She studied Paolina for a moment. "Very well then. Paolina, you will come to me after breakfast. Now it is time for Mass. I suggest you both reflect on what has happened."

During Mass Anna Maria reflected. She

sat behind Paolina, staring at the back of her head. *Papa's violin. Papa's voice.*

Suddenly she reached out and jerked Paolina's hair—hard. Paolina screamed. She turned around and glared at Anna Maria. Mass came to a halt.

Anna Maria sat with her hands in her lap and glared back.

"Girls!" said a nun at the end of the row.

"She pulled my hair!" Paolina said in a loud whisper.

"She stole my violin!" Anna Maria answered.

"Quiet!" The nun put a finger over her lips.

The priest turned back to the altar and resumed his chant.

At breakfast Anna Maria could not eat. None of the girls spoke their silent language. As they filed out of the dining room,

Silvia whispered to her. "Don't worry. Mother Elena will make her give your violin back."

Anna Maria nodded, but she was not so sure. What if Paolina had broken it in a jealous fit?

In class Maestro Vivaldi said, "I am sorry to hear what happened. But your violin will surely be found." Then he handed her Paolina's violin. "For today you may play this one."

Anna Maria shook her head. "I cannot, Maestro."

"You must, my dear," he insisted. "I know you are angry, but playing will ease your mind. Try it and see."

Anna Maria could not refuse him. She took the violin.

He nodded and looked around at the girls. "On your music stands, you will find a little exercise I wrote. I hope you practiced your *ta-ta-tas.*"

He raised his bow. "Ready?"

"*Sì,* Maestro," the girls said in unison.

He started the beat. It was true that playing made Anna Maria forget. The notes were so fast that she could think of nothing else.

When they finished, the girls were gasping or laughing. Some pretended to fall out of their chairs.

"Maestro Vivaldi, you are trying to kill us!" said one.

He laughed. "No, dear girls, just challenge you."

After class, Sister Lidia was waiting at the door. Anna Maria hurried to her. *Maybe my violin has been found,* she thought with a thrill.

But Sister Lidia was not smiling. Her blue

eyes were full of concern. "Come, Annina. Mother Elena has sent for you."

"Did she find my violin?" Anna Maria asked as they walked.

"She told me nothing, dear."

7. Confession

Mother Elena sat at her desk facing Paolina.

The prioress motioned for Anna Maria to sit. "Paolina has something to tell you."

But Anna Maria could not sit. She could not breathe. She could only stare at Paolina, who covered her face.

"Come, Paolina, tell Anna Maria what you did with her violin," Mother Elena urged.

"I threw it out the window . . . into the

canal," Paolina said. Her voice was muffled by her hands.

Anna Maria gasped and put her hand over her heart. No words would come.

"Paolina will be punished," the prioress went on. "She is suspended from classes to work in the kitchen."

Anna Maria turned and ran out of the room to the front door. She threw back the bolt and burst outside. There was Francesco, sitting in his gondola near the bridge.

"Oh, Signor Francesco, will you take me to look for my violin? That wretched Paolina threw it into this canal last night!" She took a coin from her pocket. "I can pay."

"Put away your money, *signorina.* Of course I will."

He helped her into the gondola and untied the rope. Sister Lidia and Mother Elena rushed out.

"Anna Maria, come back," called Sister Lidia.

"No! I want my violin. We're going to look for it," Anna Maria answered.

Francesco leaned into the oar. "I'll bring her back safely, Sisters," he called.

The gondola moved along below the

windows of the Pietà. Anna Maria looked from side to side. She saw nothing. Had her beloved violin sunk to the bottom of the canal?

"The tide is still in," Francesco said. "Your violin could have floated farther inland."

He rowed on, through the narrow canal.

Stone buildings rose up on either side. Finally they reached the north shore of the island, with no sign of her violin.

"Oh, Signor Francesco, I cannot live without my violin. I shall die." Anna Maria hid her face in the cushions and began to cry.

Through her sobs she heard Francesco's voice. "Why would this Paolina do such a thing, *signorina*?"

"Because she hates me," Anna Maria said into the cushions.

"And why is that?" asked Francesco.

Anna Maria sat up. "Because she is afraid I will become Maestro Vivaldi's favorite instead of her. But I hate her a thousand times more than she hates me."

Francesco said nothing. He turned the gondola back toward the Pietà. The dark waters of the canal rippled with the motion of his oar.

"I hate this canal," Anna Maria said. "I hate Venice. I hate the Pietà. I hate Paolina." She leaned against the cushions with a sigh. "I hate everything except you and your gondola and Maestro Vivaldi."

"I'm sorry you have lost your violin, *signorina.* But it is not as bad as hating everything. Without your violin you can still be a musician."

Anna Maria shook her head. "No, you don't understand. It is not just a violin. It's my father's voice."

When they came up to the bridge, Sister Lidia stood waiting for her.

"We didn't find it," Anna Maria called.

Francesco tied the gondola and helped her out. "*Signorina,* you must not lose hope."

Sister Lidia looked at Francesco. "*Signore,* you could have caused trouble for Anna Maria."

"Excuse me, Sister." He took off his red cap and bowed. "But I also could have helped find her violin. It was a risk worth taking."

Sister Lidia nodded and took Anna Maria by the hand. "Come, Annina." She started walking toward the Pietà. "My heart breaks for you, but you must not leave without permission."

Anna Maria stopped and pulled her hand away. "I don't care about the rules. I only care about my violin."

"I understand," said Sister Lidia. "But you could be removed from violin class if it happens again. Your father would not want that and neither would I."

It was true.

During supper Anna Maria stared at her plate of creamy rice. Even though she did not look at Paolina, she felt her presence.

A nun was reading from the Bible.

"Then came Peter to him, and said, 'Lord, how oft shall my brother sin against me, and I forgive him? till seven times?'"

That is for me, thought Anna Maria, *but I'll never forgive Paolina, not even once.* She covered her ears.

Silvia nudged her and pointed to the rice. *Delicious,* she mouthed.

Anna Maria nodded and took a small bite. She had to work at swallowing.

That night she lay awake as the other girls drew deep breaths of sleep. *Help me, Papa, help me. Tell me what to do.* She wept silently.

In her mind's eye she saw her violin at the bottom of the canal. Drowned. Papa's voice was gone forever. What possible hope could there be?

8. Voice in the Night

In the morning Anna Maria handed Paolina's violin to Maestro Vivaldi. "Excuse me, Maestro, I would rather not play this violin," she said.

He shook his head sadly. "That Paolina. How could she throw such an instrument into the canal?" He took a deep breath and let it out. "Well then, I must find another for you."

The next day, Maestro Vivaldi walked

into class with a violin. He set the case on a table and opened the lid. "Anna Maria, come up here, please." He took out a dark red violin. "Your father made this violin for the Pietà before you were born." He held it out to her. "I will loan it to you."

Anna Maria took the violin and embraced it. "Thank you, Maestro."

In the days that followed, she began to play the violin. But it was not the same. She could not hear Papa's voice.

Late one night Anna Maria lay awake. She listened to water lapping against the stone walls below. She got up, opened a window, and pushed back its shutters.

Moonlight danced on the water of the basin. As she watched, she heard the faint sound of a violin. *Annina,* it seemed to sing. *Annina.*

Her heart leaped. Someone in Venice was

playing her violin! She leaned out the window.

The music was coming from the west. *I have to follow it now,* she thought.

Anna Maria tiptoed to the stairs. In the dark she could see only her white nightdress. Holding on to the rail, she crept down one step at a time. She knew the front door was locked. But maybe not the chapel.

She hurried across the courtyard and opened the door. The chapel was as black as a gondola. She felt her way along the wall to the doors. Locked. She put her ear on the crack between them. Too late—the violin was quiet.

Anna Maria returned to her bed. Tomorrow she had to get out. But how? Since her last escape the front door was locked at all times. Maybe Auntie would talk to Mother Elena.

After breakfast, she waited until Sister Lidia came out of the dining room. Anna Maria took her hand and pulled her into the courtyard.

"What is it, dear child?" asked the sister.

"I have to go and look for my violin again, Auntie," said Anna Maria. "It cannot be at the bottom of the canal. I know, because I heard Papa's voice last night."

Sister Lidia put her arm around Anna Maria's shoulders. "Annina, you must have dreamed it."

Anna Maria pulled away. "No, no, no! I was standing at the window and I heard someone playing my violin."

Sister Lidia's eyebrows went up. "Where was it coming from?"

"Somewhere west of here. Please, Auntie, ask Mother Elena if we can go look for it," Anna Maria begged.

"Very well. Come with me to her office, and you can tell your story."

At the door Sister Lidia knocked. "Enter," Mother Elena said.

Anna Maria rushed to her desk. "Mother Elena, please, I beg you. Let Auntie and me go out to find my violin."

The prioress looked at Sister Lidia, then back at Anna Maria. "What are you saying, my child? Your violin is at the bottom of the canal."

Anna Maria shook her head. "No, I heard someone playing it last night."

"How very strange. Are you sure?" asked Mother Elena.

"*Sì*, Mother," Anna Maria said. "No other violin sounds like mine."

The prioress pursed her lips, thinking. "I cannot let you go running around the streets, Anna Maria. The governors have threatened to dismiss me if it happens again."

"But . . . ," Anna Maria began.

The look in Mother Elena's eyes stopped her. "Let me finish, dear child."

Anna Maria put her hand over her mouth.

"I will tell the governors your story," the prioress went on. "They will decide what is to be done."

They won't believe it, thought Anna Maria. *I must find another way.*

9. A Search

After violin class, Anna Maria waited until the other girls left.

"What is it, my dear?" Maestro Vivaldi asked.

"Oh, Maestro, last night I heard someone playing my violin," she told him. "I'm sure, because I heard Papa's voice."

The maestro's eyes widened. "Indeed!"

"Can you help?" she went on. "Mother Elena won't let me go look for it. She's going to tell the governors my story. But I don't think they will believe it."

The maestro nodded. "I will see what I can do. One of the governors owes me a favor for dedicating some music to him. Perhaps he can convince the others." Maestro Vivaldi smiled. "Especially since I shall be your escort."

Anna Maria wanted to throw her arms around him. But she dared not.

Two days later, a letter came granting the request. After classes, Maestro Vivaldi, Sister Lidia, and Anna Maria stepped out the door of the Pietà.

"I'll hire a gondola," the maestro said.

"Look!" said Anna Maria. "There is my friend, Signor Francesco."

"Good afternoon." Francesco bowed. "Where may I take you?"

"On a search," the maestro said.

"Signor Francesco," said Anna Maria, "my violin did not drown. I heard it singing in the night."

"Did I not tell you, *signorina*?" he said. "Where was the sound coming from?"

She pointed. "That direction."

Francesco turned to the maestro. "What is your wish, Don Vivaldi? Shall we wind our way through the canals and listen for it?"

"Sì," he answered.

As Francesco rowed, Anna Maria listened. She heard water rippling. She heard caged birds singing from windows. She heard a street vendor calling out his wares. But no violin.

They came to the leaning bell tower. There, a smaller canal flowed off to the right.

"Turn here, Francesco. I know of a violin shop nearby," the maestro said. "You can let us off at the next steps."

When Francesco had helped them out, he said, "I'll wait for you."

"Thank you," the maestro said. "Follow me, ladies. I don't trust this shop owner, but we will have a look."

He strode down the narrow street, his black robe flowing. Anna Maria and Sister

Lidia followed. At the open door of the shop, he waved them in.

Anna Maria looked around. There were violins hanging on the walls and lying on the counters. She saw red ones and brown ones, but not her golden violin.

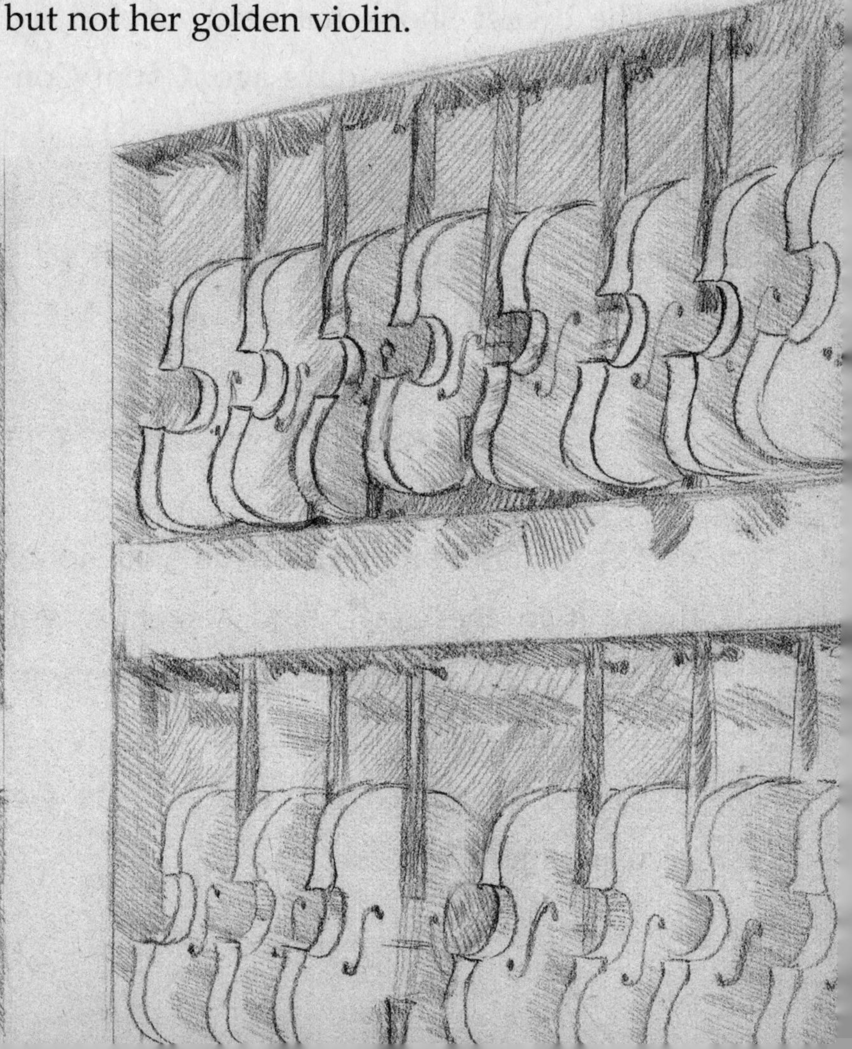

The owner, a burly man with a permanent frown, bowed. "Don Vivaldi. Are you looking for an instrument for the orphan girls?"

"*Sì,* Signor Braga," said the maestro. "One made by Nicolo Lombardini."

The owner shook his head. "I sold the only one I had three days ago. Count Contarini bought it for his daughter. He was quite taken with the violin. Especially since the master made it for his own daughter."

"That was my violin!" Anna Maria cried.

Signor Braga looked down at her. "Your violin, *signorina*?"

"*Sì,* my father made it for me. But Paolina threw it in the canal. And somehow you found it and . . . and sold it." Anger rose inside her, almost spilling out.

Signor Braga scowled at her. "Are you accusing me—"

Maestro Vivaldi held up his hand for silence. "Permit me to explain, *signore.*" He cast a look at Anna Maria that told her to keep quiet.

"This young lady is indeed Anna Maria Lombardini, daughter of Nicolo. She is also a student of mine. As you know, her father recently passed away. His last gift to her was that marvelous violin. She arrived at the Pietà clutching it to her heart."

The maestro paused. But Signor Braga said nothing.

"Unfortunately, another student became jealous. She stole the violin and threw it in the canal." Maestro Vivaldi looked steadily at the shop owner. "May I ask, *signore,* where you found it?"

Signor Braga drew a sharp breath. "I do not go about looking for violins in canals, Don Vivaldi. Nor do I sell stolen goods. The violin was brought to my shop by a fish merchant. He said someone threw it out of a window into the canal."

"It was stolen!" Anna Maria blurted.

Signor Braga made a curt bow. "I am afraid there is nothing more I can do for you." He turned and walked to the back of his shop.

10. The Contarini Palace

As Francesco rowed them home, Maestro Vivaldi turned to Anna Maria. "I once played for Count Contarini in his palace. I shall send a letter to him and ask for a meeting."

Anna Maria stood up, rocking the gondola. "Maestro, may I go with you?"

Sister Lidia held the side of the gondola and gasped.

"Signorina!" Francesco said. "Please sit down or we shall capsize."

She sat. "I'm sorry, I forgot."

Maestro Vivaldi chuckled. When the gondola stopped rocking, he went on. "You and Sister Lidia may go on one condition. You must let me do the talking."

"*Sì,* Maestro. But the count probably paid a lot of gold for my violin. How can you persuade him to give it back?"

"Leave it to me, child. I know how to deal with nobles. They all want flattery."

Two weeks later, Maestro Vivaldi received a letter from Count Contarini. He invited them to his palace the next day.

Late in the afternoon Anna Maria, the maestro, and Sister Lidia again stepped aboard Francesco's gondola. He rowed along the Riva, and into the Grand Canal.

"Watch for violins flying out of windows," Francesco said.

Anna Maria laughed out loud. "*Signore,*

you can make anything funny."

"I try," he said.

They passed palace after palace on both sides of the canal. Anna Maria saw a girl standing on a balcony and waved. The girl turned away. *People who live in palaces don't care about other people,* Anna Maria thought.

A little farther on, Maestro Vivaldi said, "There it is. The pink one on the right."

Anna Maria caught her breath. The afternoon sun cast watery reflections on the three-story marble palace. The middle floor had tall, arched windows, pointed at the top.

"I won't know how to act in such a palace," said Anna Maria. "Should I curtsy?"

"Just be yourself," said Francesco, "and the count will be charmed."

"Curtsy when I do," said Sister Lidia.

"And let me do the talking," said Maestro Vivaldi.

Anna Maria nodded and kept her mouth tightly closed.

Francesco pulled up to the steps and helped the three of them out. "Good luck."

"Thank you," said Anna Maria. "We'll need it."

Maestro Vivaldi rang the bell while Anna Maria peered through the gate. A long room reached all the way to the other side of the palace. The only light came from openings at either end. An elderly servant appeared, shuffling along the tile floor.

"Don Antonio Vivaldi to see Count Contarini, please," said the maestro.

"Ah, Don Vivaldi." The man opened the gate and bowed. "It is a pleasure to see you again. Please, follow me."

Anna Maria glanced back at Francesco, who stood beside his gondola. He curtsied like a lady. She had to hold in a giggle.

They climbed marble steps up to the first floor and entered another long room. This one was flooded with light from the tall, pointed windows. Straight chairs lined the walls around Persian rugs.

"Please, sit down," said the old man. "I will tell the count you are here."

Anna Maria sat on one of the chairs between the maestro and Sister Lidia. She looked up. The ceiling was painted blue, with fluffy clouds and angels flying up to heaven. It was like being in a church.

"When I played here, the countess swooned in delight," said Maestro Vivaldi.

Just then Count Contarini entered the room. He was a tall man with dark curling hair. "I remember that, Don Vivaldi."

Anna Maria's heart fell. He was not smiling. Nor did he have the violin in hand.

Maestro Vivaldi stood up and bowed.

"Excellency, it has been too long since I played for your illustrious family. I trust you will not deny me the pleasure of returning soon, that I may entertain you with my feeble efforts."

Count Contarini squinted at the maestro. But he said nothing.

"Speaking of feeble efforts," the maestro went on, "it would give me great joy to dedicate my newest concerto to your noble self."

Anna Maria had never heard Maestro Vivaldi talk like this. *Feeble efforts?* Everyone loved his music. Was this what he meant by flattery?

Maestro Vivaldi bowed again. "Of course that which I offer is a small tribute—"

"Let us speak frankly, Don Vivaldi," the count interrupted. "Am I to understand that I have purchased a stolen violin?"

The maestro sucked in a breath and held

it for a moment. Then he gestured to Anna Maria and Sister Lidia.

"Excellency, may I present Anna Maria Lombardini, daughter of the great violin maker. And her chaperone, Sister Lidia."

Anna Maria watched Sister Lidia and curtsied when she did.

The count dipped his head in a bow. "So you are Annina."

"*Sì*, Excellency," Anna Maria said. Then she clamped her lips together.

A brief smile crossed his face. But it faded as he turned to Maestro Vivaldi. "Of course I had no idea the violin had been stolen. I paid many gold coins for it as a gift to my daughter. Even now she is having a lesson."

He spoke to the old servant. "Please ask Donata to come and bring her violin."

They waited in silence until Donata entered. She was a thin, dark-haired girl—her father's image. She held the golden instrument in her arms.

"My violin!" Anna Maria took a step toward her.

Donata fled from the room.

Anna Maria clasped her hand over her mouth. Had she ruined everything?

"I apologize for my daughter's rude manners," the count said. "She is quite fond of the violin."

"And I apologize for Anna Maria," said Sister Lidia. "She, too, is quite fond of the violin."

Anna Maria wanted to hug Auntie for that.

"No doubt," said the count. "But I am sure you understand that my daughter comes first. I will not ask her to give up the violin."

Anna Maria stared at Count Contarini, at his thin face and his hard black eyes. This man stood between her and Papa's violin. Her eyes brimmed with tears. She put her face in her hands.

She could not let this happen. In that moment she heard Papa's voice in her head. *Annina, play for me.* A bold idea came to her. Maestro Vivaldi could do the talking. But she could do the playing.

She looked up at the count, blinking away her tears. "Excellency, may I play the violin one last time?"

He smiled. "*Sì,* of course." He spoke to the old servant again. "Tell Donata that Anna Maria wishes to play the violin one last time."

Donata returned and handed the violin to her father. She stood watching as he gave it to Anna Maria.

The violin felt warm and alive in her hands. She tucked it under her chin and tuned.

"What will you play for us?" the count asked.

"The piece my father asked me to play when he lay on his deathbed," Anna Maria said.

There was a stunned silence.

Anna Maria raised the bow, closed her eyes, and drew in a breath.

Dum dee-dee dum . . . , she played. Her heart seemed to grow and fill her chest. *An-ni-na, An-ni-na,* the violin sang to her. She wanted to go on playing and never stop.

At the end Anna Maria let her bow arm drop to her side. She saw that Count Contarini's eyes shone with tears.

He said, "Don Vivaldi, that is beautiful. With respect, you should keep to composing music rather than speeches."

A smile spread across the maestro's face. "Not all nobles really listen to music as you do, Excellency. If they did, I would not have to make speeches."

The count nodded. Then to Anna Maria he said, "I am deeply moved by your playing, *signorina.* You and the violin seem as one." He turned to his daughter.

Her face twisted with the struggle going on inside her head. At last she spoke to Anna Maria. "My father gave me this violin one night at dinner. Afterward I went out on the balcony and played it by moonlight."

"I heard you!" said Anna Maria. "From my window in the Pietà."

"I loved the violin," Donata went on. "But it felt restless in my hands. As I played, I knew that its spirit belonged to Annina. Wherever she might be."

Donata paused and looked at the count. "May I, Father?"

He nodded.

"And so, my father and I agree that the violin is yours to keep," Donata said. "You belong together."

Anna Maria opened her mouth, but no words came out. She ran to Donata and hugged her.

Then Anna Maria stepped back. "Count Contarini, how can I ever repay you?"

He smiled. "You just did, *signorina*."

11. Paolina

On the way home, Francesco said, "And what of Paolina? Shall we toss her in the canal?"

Anna Maria burst out laughing.

"*Signorina,* do you remember what I told you when you first arrived here?"

"*Sì,* no one can be sad in Venice. At least not for long."

Francesco nodded. "I think Paolina must be sad for what she did."

"Truly?" said Anna Maria.

"*Sì.* And I think you are the only person who can make her happy," he went on.

Now that she had her violin back, Anna Maria wanted everyone to be happy. "How, Signor Francesco?"

"I can't tell you how, *signorina.*"

"Francesco, you should have been a priest," said the maestro.

"Oh no, Don Vivaldi. They would have unfrocked me by now. Besides, I prefer the open air." And with that Francesco began to sing.

A woman standing on a balcony sang with him.

"Ah, Venice," said Maestro Vivaldi. He glanced at Sister Lidia, who blushed.

That evening at vespers Anna Maria escaped to the courtyard with her violin. The plum trees were in white flower. She inhaled their perfume. Then she closed her eyes and began to play. Her spirit soared with Papa's voice.

When Anna Maria opened her eyes, she saw Paolina peeking out from behind a column. Quickly she disappeared.

"Paolina, is that you?" Anna Maria called in a loud whisper.

Paolina stepped out from behind the column and walked toward Anna Maria. She looked thinner, and her stringy hair was tangled.

She stopped a few feet away. "Is that your violin?"

"Sì," said Anna Maria. She told Paolina everything that had happened.

"It is a miracle," Paolina said. She covered her face with her hands. "I don't know how I could do such a thing. You must hate me."

"Not anymore," said Anna Maria.

Paolina looked up. "Why? Because you have your violin back?"

"Sì, but also because of what my friend the gondolier said. He thinks you are sad for what you did."

Paolina stared at the paving stones and nodded. "Your friend is right. I am sad . . . and sorry, too."

"Then I will sing you a song he taught me. It made me laugh, even when I was sad about my father."

Anna Maria took up her violin. "It goes like this."

"If macaroni rained down from the sky,
And the earth were covered over with cheese,
We'd use our oars as forks, you and I.
How jolly! Macaroni raining down
from the sky!"

Paolina laughed, but her eyes were still sad.

"You must miss violin class," said Anna Maria.

"*Sì,* Maestro Vivaldi was like a father to

me." Paolina sighed. "If only I could be back in his class."

"Why don't we ask him?" Anna Maria said. "He's probably still here."

"But I'm not allowed upstairs," Paolina said.

"I won't tell. We can sneak up there while everyone is at vespers." Anna Maria put her violin back in its case.

Then the two girls hurried along the gallery to the stairway door. All was quiet. They ran up the stairs to the music room.

Anna Maria stepped inside with Paolina right behind her. The maestro did not see or hear them. He set his violin down on the table and began to write.

The girls stood frozen by the door. At last he laid the quill pen aside and sat back. It was then that the maestro saw them.

"Do my eyes play tricks on me?" he said.

"I am sorry to interrupt you, Maestro," said Anna Maria.

"Dear girl, no one can do that. But tell me, is it possible that you two have made peace?" he asked.

"*Sì*, Maestro," said Anna Maria. "And we have come to ask you a favor."

"What might that be?"

Anna Maria glanced at Paolina, then back at Maestro Vivaldi. "Paolina is truly sad for what she did."

"I am glad to hear it," he said.

Anna Maria took courage. "Would you let her return to violin class, Maestro?"

He studied Paolina for a time.

She looked down. "I am ashamed, Maestro Vivaldi."

"Very good. I will see what I can do." He stood, put away his violin, and gathered up his papers. "In two weeks we shall perform my Concerto in G Minor. It is for two violins and cello. Silvia will play the cello part. And I think I know the two violinists."

Anna Maria gasped. Her first concert, and the maestro wanted her to play a solo!

"You can do it—both of you—but it will be hard work. I shall hand out the music tomorrow." He nodded and walked out the door.

12. Finale

The girls of the orchestra filed into the chapel balcony. Anna Maria could see that every seat in the audience was taken. In the front row sat the doge in his robe and pointed hat. Senators sat on either side of him. Count Contarini, the countess, and Donata were just behind. Toward the back she saw Francesco.

Anna Maria put her hand over her racing heart and whispered to Paolina, "I'm so nervous."

"So am I, but take deep breaths," Paolina said.

Silvia leaned close. "Think only of the music."

Maestro Vivaldi strode in and took his place. He raised his hands and looked at each of the soloists. Then he started the beat. On her cello Silvia began the deep, slow bowing. *Dum—dum—dum—dum.* Soon the violin section joined in. The four beats went on, rising and falling again.

Now it was time for the two violins. Anna Maria could hear the maestro's voice in her head. *Together now, let your violins sing the melody.*

She glanced at Paolina, and they began. Anna Maria forgot the audience. She let herself be carried along on the music.

When the galloping final movement ended, the audience began to make a racket. They scraped their feet on the floor and coughed. They blew their noses with loud snorts. Francesco swayed from side to side as he stomped his feet.

"Clapping is not allowed in the chapel," Paolina told her. "So all that noise means they loved us."

Anna Maria looked at Maestro Vivaldi.

"*Brava,* dear girls, *brava!*" he said.

Anna Maria felt her heart swell. *Francesco was right,* she thought. *I can be happy in Venice. And Papa was right to send me to the Pietà. Here I can be a musician.*

No longer did it seem like a prison. It was a school and a home, with a mother, an aunt, many sisters . . . and a red-haired father.

Glossary

basilica [buh-SILL-ih-kuh]: early Christian church

brava [BRAH-vah]: well done

doge [dohj]: chief government official of Venice

don [dohn]: title for a highly respected man

gondola [GON-duh-luh]: long, narrow Venetian boat

gondolier [gon-duh-LEER]: person who rows a gondola

illustrious [ih-LUS-tree-us]: very famous

lagoon [luh-GOON]: shallow body of water connected to a larger one

largo [LAR-go]: slow part of a musical composition

lire [LEE-reh]: monetary units of Italy

maestro [MY-stroh]: title for a conductor,

composer, or teacher of music

Mass: church service that celebrates Communion

Pietà [pee-ay-TAH]: name of an orphanage in Venice

prioress [PRY-uh-russ]: head nun

quill: feather writing pen

sì [see]: yes

signor/e [seen-YOHR/eh]: mister

signorina [seen-yuh-REE-nuh]: miss

unfrock [un-FRAHK]: take away one's priestly duties

vespers [VES-purz]: evening worship service

Historical Note

It may seem odd that an orphanage would also be a music school. Indeed, the Pietà was one of four orphanages in Venice. They competed with one another to have the best music teachers, students, and performances.

The Pietà began as a regular orphanage. There were classes in reading, writing, and arithmetic. The girls also learned embroidery, lace making, sewing, spinning, and weaving. Their work was sold to help support the orphanage.

Venice was a city of music lovers. Someone realized that the orphan girls who showed musical talent could become musicians. They could earn money for the orphanage by giving performances. Most of the girls had no family name. So each was given the name of the instrument she played, such as Silvia of the Cello.

The Pietà was fortunate to have Antonio Vivaldi. He taught violin and other stringed instruments. He composed music for the girls and conducted the orchestra. Because of Vivaldi, this group of young musicians became famous. People, even kings, came from all over Europe to see and hear the orphan girls perform.

Although Anna Maria is a fictional girl, she could be real. The idea that her violin held her father's soul and voice was inspired by the great violin maker Antonio Stradivari. He liked to keep each violin in his bedroom for a month before varnishing it. He believed his soul entered the violin while he slept. And he should know!